The Pet Sitter

JULIE SYKES

ILLUSTRATED BY
NATHAN REED

DiXiE IN DANGER

For Alistair, Will, Tim and Antonia

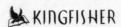

KINGFISHER

First published 2009 by Kingfisher
an imprint of Macmillan Children's Books
a division of Macmillan Publishers Limited
20 New Wharf Road, London N1 9RR
Basingstoke and Oxford
Associated companies throughout the world
www.panmacmillan.com

ISBN 978-0-7534-1637-2

3 5 7 9 8 6 4 2
1TR/1108/MCK/(PICA)/60HLM/C

A CIP catalogue record for this book is available from the British Library.

Printed and Bound in the UK by CPI Mackays, Chatham ME5 8TD

CONTENTS

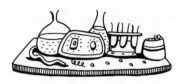

CHAPTER ONE
AN EMERGENCY

Max raced in from the garden and through the back door, where he snatched at the ringing phone.

'Max?' said an impatient voice. 'Max, the pet sitter?'

'Yes,' said Max.

Max had been pet-sitting for a while now and had looked after some unusual animals for some very strange owners.

'This is an emergency,' the voice continued. 'I have to go away right now and I need someone to take care of my pet dormouse. Her name's Dixie. Can you do it?'

'Sure,' said Max, checking his watch. He was looking after a troupe of zebra fish and they were due a dancing lesson at three thirty, but there was plenty of time to go and meet Dixie first. 'What's your name and where do you live?'

'I'm Ivor, Ivor Gadget, and I live at 36 Sandy Road. Look, this really is an emergency. Can you come straight away?'

'Already left!' said Max cheerfully, hanging up.

Max went upstairs to get his pet sitter's notebook. This was a small hardback book with a picture of a whale on the cover. In it

Max wrote down the names of the animals he was pet-sitting and notes on their care. Max kept his notebook buried in his sock drawer. It was a simple but safe hiding place. Alice, his bossy big sister, was always nosing into his business. But she wouldn't dream of touching his socks, not for anything!

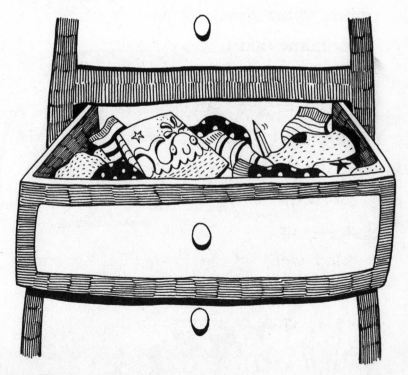

Max shoved the notebook and a pencil in his pocket, then ran downstairs to the garden. Alice had gone outside to practise her dance moves; her legs were everywhere and her bottom stuck up in the air. Max couldn't help himself. It was time to get Alice back for telling on him yesterday when he accidently glued the TV remote control to the lounge carpet.

Max gave her bottom a small shove, then legged it as Alice toppled head first into the snapdragons.

'Max!' she shrieked. 'I'll get you for that!'

'You'll have to catch me first,' said Max, running into the garden shed. He was on his bike and cycling up the garden before Alice was back on her feet.

'Whatever is going on?' asked Mum,

coming out of the back door. 'Why is Alice sitting in the flowers?'

'Perhaps she thinks they'll make her smell nicer,' chuckled Max. 'I'm going out. I've got another job.'

'Not so fast, young man. Where and who?'

'Aw, Mum!' Max stopped a safe distance

from Alice, who was mouthing threats at him. 'Sandy Road, number 36. Ivor Gadget wants me to look after his dormouse.'

'A dormouse!' exclaimed Mum. 'I've never heard of keeping a pet dormouse. Oh well, have fun and be back by teatime.'

'I will,' said Max. 'Thanks, Mum. Bye, Alice.'

He waved at his sister. It felt good to get the better of her for a change!

Sandy Road wasn't far, and as Max pedalled along he tried to imagine what sort of person kept a dormouse. They weren't exactly challenging animals. From what Max could remember, dormice were nocturnal and spent up to three-quarters of their life asleep.

'I bet Ivor Gadget is ancient,' Max panted. 'That's why he's got a dormouse.

He'll be an old man with grey hair and wrinkles.'

Max turned the corner of Sandy Road and looked at the house numbers. The evens were on his left-hand side and he counted them off.

'30 . . . 32 . . . 34 . . . there it is!'

Number 36 was slightly different from the other houses. Instead of having a small brick wall, the front garden was surrounded by a high fence. Max parked his bike and looked for a gate, but there wasn't one. The fence stretched in an unbroken line the whole way around the house. So how did he get in? Carefully Max studied the fence. It was very high, but he was good at climbing. Max thought if he stood on the next-door neighbour's brick wall he could easily climb over. Max spat on his hands, then wiped

them down his shorts to give himself better grip. He scrambled on to the brick wall, but as he reached up to the fence he heard a sharp click followed by a whirring noise. Looking up, Max 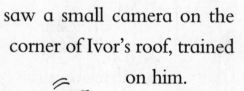 saw a small camera on the corner of Ivor's roof, trained on him.

'Name?' asked a metallic voice.

Suspiciously Max stared at the camera. Was this a wind-up?

'Name?' repeated the voice impatiently.

'Max. Max Barker, the pet sitter.'

'Welcome, Max Barker.'

There was a louder click, and a gate cleverly hidden in the fence swung open.

Max stared in amazement. 'Cool!' he said.

'Hurry up,' said the camera crossly. 'I haven't got all day.'

'Nor have I!' Max grabbed his bicycle and pushed it through the gate.

He was barely inside when the gate slammed shut and a second camera, mounted above the front door, focused its lens on him.

'Name?' said the camera, in a squeaky metallic voice.

'What? Again?'

'No name, no entry.'

'Max Barker. I'm here to pet-sit. I

thought this was an emergency!'

The front door opened so suddenly that Max almost fell inside.

'It is. Don't mind the cameras. They're a bit too enthusiastic at times. I'm Ivor. Thanks for coming so quickly.'

'Oh!' exclaimed Max, staring up.

Ivor Gadget was not the wrinkled old man Max had imagined. He was young and tall and wore his long brown hair loosely tied in a ponytail. Ivor glanced around, then quickly pulled Max inside, slamming the door behind him.

'Sorry about the security. I'm an inventor, if you hadn't already guessed. You wouldn't believe the trouble I've had with people trying to steal my ideas. But enough of me. Come and meet Dixie. You're going to love her!'

CHAPTER TWO
DIXIE VILLA

Max followed Ivor along the hall to a room at the back of the house. On the way he passed a lift-like door with a strip of red-and-white plastic tape stretched across it. A sign on the door read, 'Out of Order. Do NOT Enter.'

'What's that?' asked Max curiously. 'Is it a lift?'

Ivor looked shifty.

'Latest invention,' he mumbled. 'It's not finished.'

'What does it do?' asked Max.

Ivor stopped and turned to face him.

'No questions!' he said dramatically. 'Look, I'm going to have to ask you to sign the Ivor Gadget Secrecy Pact. Anything you see or hear about this house is strictly private. You mustn't tell anyone. Not an earwig!'

'I won't say a thing,' said Max, pretending to zip up his mouth. 'Am I signing in blood?'

'No need for that,' said Ivor. 'An ink pen will be fine. Providing it's not invisible ink of course!' He laughed.

Max laughed too. He'd only been joking about the blood!

'Here we are,' said Ivor, opening a door. 'Come and meet Dixie.'

Ivor ushered Max into the room. Max

stopped inside the door and stared in amazement. The room was even more messy than Alice's bedroom, and that was saying something! Tall bookcases lined the room and were crammed with everything from books to old bicycle wheels. The floor was covered with teetering piles of more books and mountains of cogs, wires, nuts, bolts, screws, computer bits and reels of sticky tape. Ivor wove his way through the junk to the table.

'Dixie Villa,' he said grandly.

'Wow!' Max exclaimed.

The cage looked like a two storey doll's house, but with a wire mesh front and a glass conservatory instead of a roof on top. Max peered through the mesh at the front rooms. Each one looked like an overgrown garden in miniature. The long grass was peppered with wild flowers, shaggy bushes and brambles. Max pushed his little finger through the mesh.

'Wicked!' he exclaimed. 'It's real.'

'Dixie likes the best of both words,' said Ivor, smiling at Max's astonishment. 'That's her natural environment, then there's the conservatory up top.'

A wooden staircase, carpeted with soft green moss, led to the all-glass conservatory. In contrast to the garden rooms the conservatory housed a huge gymnasium with three brightly coloured tunnels to slide down, a treadmill, weights, an exercise

bicycle and a climbing wall. A small dormouse, wearing green sweatbands around her head and paws, was pounding away on the treadmill. Suddenly the machine slowed, then it stopped and Dixie jumped off.

'Hello,' said Max, gently tapping on the glass.

Dixie fixed Max with her big black eyes. Then she turned her back on him.

'Dixie!' said Ivor, in a warning tone.

The little dormouse totally ignored him and hopped towards the stairs.

'Dixie,' said Ivor again, 'come and meet Max Barker, the pet sitter.'

Dixie reached the top of the staircase and hesitated.

'Max is going to look after you for the next three days. I know you don't want to stay here on your own, but it's not Max's fault so come and say hello.'

Ivor turned apologetically to Max, 'Dixie's not used to being locked inside her villa. Usually she comes and goes as she pleases.'

Dixie sat watching Ivor as if she was listening to him. When he'd finished she fluffed out her orange-brown fur and stared at Ivor with big eyes. Max held his breath. Dixie looked so sad he thought she might be going to cry!

'Dixie, don't!' Ivor
pleaded. 'I've made up
my mind – you're staying
here while I go abroad.'

Dixie thumped her long
furry tail on the ground,
then, shooting an angry
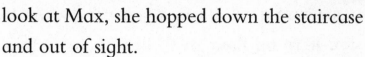
look at Max, she hopped down the staircase
and out of sight.

'She likes me then!' said Max.

'It's not you,' said Ivor hurriedly. 'It's me
she's cross with. I've never left her before
and, as I said, I've never locked her up either.'

'I don't mind if you don't lock her cage,'
said Max.

'It's not that simple,' said Ivor shiftily.
'Dixie's a live wire. She's always up to
mischief. I don't want her messing with my
inventions.'

He checked his watch.

'Widgets! Look at the time! I've got a plane to catch. I was lucky to get a seat – it was a last-minute cancellation. Quick, come to the kitchen. So much to do! There's the secrecy pact to sign, and your money to sort out. I'll show you what to feed Dixie and . . . Oops, I almost forgot! I need to do a scan of your eye.'

CHAPTER THREE
A NASTY SHOCK

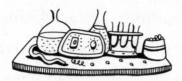

Cycling along to Ivor Gadget's early the next morning, Max reminded himself of his pet-sitting duties. Ivor had left all Dixie's favourite foods. There was a bag of hazelnuts, a jar of sunflower seeds, raspberries and apricots. It seemed an awful lot for such a small creature, but Ivor said that Dixie had a good appetite. Max had also brought Dixie a bunch of honeysuckle freshly cut from his garden. Last night, reading up about dormice, Max discovered they liked to shred it up and sleep in it. He hoped the present might cheer Dixie up. She hadn't seemed too happy yesterday.

Max reached the start of Ivor's fence and climbed off his bike.

'One, two, three, four,' he counted.

When he'd taken twelve footsteps he stopped, turned to face the fence and then counted six hands up from the bottom. Keeping his hand on the fence, Max crouched down until his eyes were level with his hand. Then, pulling it away, he stared at the fence. There it was! The tiny hole Ivor had told him about yesterday. There was a click, Max blinked and the hidden gate swung open.

'That is so neat!' Max exclaimed.

Instead of a key, the doors opened by recognizing people's eyes. Yesterday Ivor had scanned the inside of Max's eye so that he could get in too.

Leaving his bicycle just inside the gate Max repeated the whole thing at the front door shouting, 'Hi, Dixie. It's only me,' as he stepped inside.

The house had an empty feel. Maybe Dixie was still asleep. Max hurried down the hall, glancing curiously at the lift-like door as he passed. It was an odd thing to have in a home, and Max wondered what it was for. Pushing open the door to Dixie's room, Max threaded his way round the piles of junk. Dixie Villa seemed even more impressive this morning. Max decided Ivor must be very fond of the dormouse to build her such an amazing home. Dixie was not in the gym or any of the front rooms. Max lay the honeysuckle on the table in front of Dixie Villa and called out,

'Hi, Dixie. It's Max.'

Nothing, not even a friendly squeak! The silence worried Max.

'Dixie, are you in there? It's breakfast time. Come and say hello and then I'll get you something to eat. I wonder what you'd like? How about an apricot with some raspberries?'

There was still no sign of Dixie.

'Good choice. Apricot it is then,' said Max, reaching out to unclip the tiny water bottle fastened to the outside of Dixie's cage.

The bottle had a small metal drinking spout that poked through the cage bars.

Max was lifting it out when the spout whipped round and blasted him with cold water.

'Eeek!' he shrieked, dropping the bottle on the table. 'How the flip did that happen?' Wiping the water from his eyes, Max was sure he heard a squeaky giggle.

'Ouch!'

Something pinged him on the nose. It was

a sunflower seed and it was quickly followed by more. Max scrabbled around, picking them up and flicking them back. It was a waste of time. Dixie  was too well hidden in the overgrown garden for the seeds to hit her, but Max enjoyed flicking the seeds all the same.

After a bit the missiles stopped. Over the top of a small bush came a twig with a white flower speared on the end.

'Truce,' shouted a squeaky voice.

Max stared in amazement as Dixie slowly peeked out from behind the bush.

A talking dormouse! Was this a trick too?

'Truce,' said Dixie crossly. 'Are you deaf or what?'

Max recovered himself.

'No, I just didn't realize that you could talk. You never said a word yesterday when Ivor was here.'

'There was nothing to say,' said Dixie. 'Truce? Will you stop fighting me?'

'You started it!' Max exclaimed.

'It's not my fault.'

'Well, it wasn't mine!'

'Being locked up is doing funny things to me. I'm going mad in here. You've got to let me out.'

Dixie's long black whiskers quivered. Max held his breath as she slowly edged out into the open. Her bright black eyes were sad, 'Please?' she said.

'Dixie, I can't do that. Ivor said I was to keep you locked up for your own safety.'

'Pooey!' exclaimed Dixie. 'I never mess with any of his inventions! Make them better, yes. Invent stuff Ivor's not even thought of, yes. But mess things up? No, NEVER!'

Max was torn. Dixie was used to having her freedom, and it felt mean to cage her, but Max was responsible for her safety. What if he disobeyed Ivor and something went wrong – how would he feel then?

'It's only for three days. You'll be out before you know it. I'll spend the daytime with you, if you like. Keep you company.'

'Pooey! I'd rather keep my own company,' Dixie growled.

'Suit yourself,' said Max. 'The offer stands, if you change your mind. I'll get your breakfast.'

He picked up the water bottle from the table.

'Neat trick, by the way. How did you get it to squirt me?'

Dixie didn't answer. Sighing to himself, Max took the bottle along to the kitchen to refill it. Ivor had left the apricots in a bowl and Max gently squeezed them, choosing the softest for Dixie's breakfast. He cut it in half, removed the stone and piled fresh raspberries on top. The whole thing looked so tasty that Max could have eaten it himself. He washed his sticky hands before proudly carrying the water and food back to Dixie.

'Breakfast, and I brought you some honeysuckle too.'

31

Max hadn't expected an answer, but when he looked through the cage he got a nasty shock. Dixie lay on her side in the long grass, eyes closed, tail stuck out like a flag pole. She was very still. Too still. Max stepped closer.

CHAPTER FOUR
THE CHASE

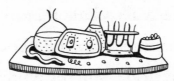

'Dixie? Dixie, are you all right?'

Max threw down her breakfast and wrenched open the front of the cage. A jumble of thoughts whizzed through his mind. Dixie was so still she didn't seem to be breathing. Had she died? But how? She'd been fine a few minutes ago. Unless the upset had given her a heart attack. Max thought he was having one too. His heart was jumping like a kangaroo. What should he do? Last term at school, Max's class had been taught how to give mouth-to-mouth resuscitation. It was a way of breathing for someone if they couldn't do it for themselves. Could you give a dormouse mouth-to-mouth? Max decided to try. He knew to be careful. Dixie was so little that if he breathed too hard she might blow up like a balloon!

Dixie lay stone still as with trembling fingers Max reached inside the cage to lift her out. His fingers touched her thick orange fur. Thwap! Dixie smacked Max with her tail.

'Sucker!' she squeaked, jumping up and leaping to freedom.

'Dixie!' bellowed Max. 'That's not funny.'

Dixie scampered across the table, scattering the bunch of honeysuckle as she ran down to the floor. Max leaped after her, knocking over piles of junk in his rush to stop her from escaping. He would have caught her if he hadn't tripped over a broken guitar that sent him crashing to the ground.

'Mouse brains!' said Max, pulling his foot from the hole in the middle. The guitar's broken strings snaked round his legs, holding him tightly. Max pulled them away, then scrambled after Dixie. He was in time to see her fat orange tail disappear around the bend in the stairs. Max climbed up after her and found himself in a room even more cluttered than the one he'd just left.

'Dixie?'

Max leaned against the door frame and scanned the messy room. And his mum thought she had problems with Alice! You could hide a rhinoceros in here and nobody would ever know.

'Come on, Dixie. The joke's over.'

Dixie didn't answer. No surprises there then!

There was another lift-like door in this room, with a single strip of red-and-white plastic tape across it. Max did some quick calculating. It was directly above the one downstairs. So it was a lift! He noticed a

keypad to the side of the door, with two large buttons marked P and F. What did that mean? Max grinned. Inventors! They were all the same. Two cakes short of a party!

There was a rustle from the other side of the room. Max spun around. The noise had come from under the window. Silently he tiptoed towards it. Suddenly an orange ball of fur broke cover and shot across the room towards the door. Turning, Max dived, his fingers closing around Dixie's tail as he landed.

'Gotcha!'

But he hadn't! Max was left holding a clump of soft orange fur as Dixie scampered away. There followed a crazy chase – Dixie whizzing around the room, Max crashing after her through mounds of junk. Max was determined to catch Dixie and dived like a footballer each time the dormouse popped into sight. A bead of sweat ran down his nose, and his heart was banging like mad. He paused for a moment to catch his breath, then leaped up as Dixie shot past. Halfway across the room Dixie disappeared in a bundle of old clothes. The clothes jumped and wriggled like live things, then suddenly stopped moving. Max crept closer. A stripy jumper caught his eye. Was that a dormouse-shaped bump in its sleeve? Silently Max squatted down. Yes, he was sure it was Dixie! Max prodded the bump. The jumper squeaked and the bump ran down its sleeve. Max cupped his hands and as Dixie ran out through the cuff he sprang.

'Gotcha!' he cried.

He skidded across

the floor, crashed through the red plastic tape and smacked into the lift buttons. The lift door sprang open and Max hurtled inside, letting Dixie go as he rolled across the floor. Dixie struggled up, then stared around in horror.

'Quick!' she squeaked. 'We've got to get out of here!'

The lift doors were closing.

Dixie ran towards them shrieking, 'Out, NOW!'

Max could see they wouldn't make it in time so he looked for a button to keep the doors open. All lifts had them, so where was it? He ran his hands across the wall in case he was missing something and found a crease in the surface. He felt it with his finger. The crease made a square with an indent at the top. Max stuck his finger into the indent and pulled. The square of wall opened, revealing the lift's controls: four buttons and a circular hole with a wire poking out. The buttons were marked with P, F, <> and ><. The symbols were the same as the ones in the lift at the shopping centre. Max couldn't guess what the P and F meant but he knew that <> would open the doors and >< would close them.

The lift doors snapped shut. Frantically Max pushed the button marked <> but it was too late. The lift was moving.

CHAPTER FIVE
A RIDE IN A LIFT

They were going up, which was strange as Ivor's house only had two floors. After a few seconds the lift stopped. Relieved, Max pressed the button to open the doors, and when nothing happened he pressed it again. Without warning the lift threw itself sideways. Max grabbed for the handrail and was glad he had. Now the lift was spinning, faster and faster, making his skinny body shake and his teeth chatter together.

'Hold on,' shouted Dixie, climbing on to

Max's foot and sinking her claws into his shoelace.

'Great idea!' said Max, like he was going to do anything else! He was spinning so violently that he could hardly breathe. He wanted to pick Dixie up, make sure she was safe, but when he tried he found the force was too great and he couldn't move.

The spinning went on until Max could hardly bear it, then at last the lift slowed and finally stopped moving. 'Whoa!' said Max. He stood for a

second, too giddy to move, but then as he reached up to open the doors . . .

'Eek!'

Faster than a stone hurled from the top of a tower block, the lift plummeted. Max's stomach met his feet, then suddenly, without even slowing, the lift stopped again. Max almost bit his tongue as it bounced up and down like it had landed on an enormous trampoline. Up and down went the lift, until gradually it stopped and the doors slid open.

'Dixie, are you OK?'

There was a muffled squeak. Dixie was clinging on to Max's shoelace with her teeth as well as both his front paws. Max staggered through the doors blinking in the bright light. 'That,' he said, 'was some ride!'

'Don't mind me,' Dixie squeaked crossly. She jumped from Max's foot. 'Call yourself a pet sitter! You nearly squashed me with those thumping great feet.'

'Sorry!' Max bent down to pick her up, but she slapped him off with her tail.

'You will be,' she exclaimed. 'Ivor's going to kill you when he finds out you've taken his lift. You're the one that needs locking up. Not me!'

'What! This is your fault!' said Max hotly. 'I'm only here because I was chasing you. Where are we, anyway? Is this Ivor's garden?'

He looked around and saw neatly trimmed hedges, colourful plants, stone statues, a rectangular pond with a dolphin fountain in the middle and mosaic around the edge.

'Nice,' said Max, 'if you like that sort of thing. Bit too Ancient Rome for me. There's nowhere to kick a ball.'

'Ancient Rome?' asked Dixie.

'Yep, we did it in history last term. We had a Roman Britain day and wore tunics a bit like that boy over there . . .' Max's voice trailed away.

'Hide,' hissed Dixie, diving under a bush.

Max wriggled after her. The boy was in a hurry and luckily didn't notice the lift nestled between two small willowy trees. He muttered to himself as he struggled to carry a huge basket full of ripe cherries. Max's stomach rumbled. Breakfast seemed a long time ago.

Dixie, who hadn't eaten her breakfast, was

obviously thinking the same thing. 'Come on,' she said, once the boy had passed. 'Let's go and find where those cherries came from.'

'Hang on!' said Max. 'Dixie, where are we exactly?'

'Not too sure,' said Dixie. 'Roman Britain sounds about right. Impossible to say without looking at the time dial.'

'You're saying that's a time lift!' squeaked Max. 'I don't believe you!'

'Excuse me, did I say time lift? Silly me! I meant we've taken the lift to Ivor's attic. Look around, bright eyes. What do you see?'

Max stuck his head out of the bush and gazed around, noticing a low villa with high windows and a veranda on the other side of the pond. Just then two girls in short white tunics hurried up the garden with a basket of tomatoes and disappeared inside the house.

'It is Roman Britain!' Max exclaimed. 'Unreal!'

'Well I'm real and I need food,' said Dixie. 'Come on.'

Max hesitated. The responsible pet-sitter

side of him said to get back into the lift and go straight home. But the curious, adventure-seeking side was dying to see a bit more of Roman Britain.

'Hurry up,' said Dixie. 'You'll think better on a full stomach.'

Max crumpled. The cherries had looked delicious. Surely it wouldn't hurt to have a little look around? It was the chance of a lifetime, and he'd regret it if he didn't take it. He scrambled out of the bush and hurried after Dixie.

'What did you mean about thinking better on a full stomach?' he asked.

Dixie didn't answer and Max got the feeling she was hiding something, but before

he could question her they reached the orchard.

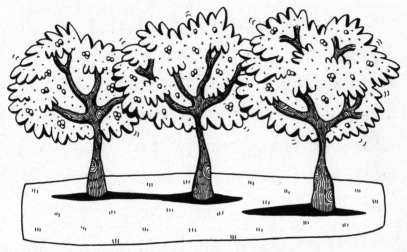

'Wow!' said Max, impressed by the fruit-laden trees. 'Where shall we start?'

CHAPTER SIX
DIXIE DISAPPEARS

A short ladder was propped against one tree, and next to it was a huge basket full of shiny red cherries. Dixie scampered up the side of the basket and began eating. Max had never picked cherries before so he climbed halfway up the ladder and ate them straight from the tree. They tasted delicious! Sticky sweet juice squirted over him as he bit into the soft flesh. He was so busy eating, and seeing how far he could spit the stones, that he didn't hear the soft steps approaching. He nearly fell off the

ladder in surprise when a voice shouted up at him,

'Don't let the master catch you. He'll chop your hand off for that.'

Max's stomach clenched. Suddenly the fruit tasted sour in his mouth.

'You're new, aren't you? Where are you from? You must be foreign with clothes like that!'

'I'm not the one wearing the dress!' Max exclaimed.

The boy gave him an odd look.

'There's no need to be unfriendly.'

'I wasn't,' said Max, trying not to laugh.

Max always laughed

when he was nervous, and it often got him into trouble. 'I'm British,' he added.

'You must be from up north then. I hear they're a barbaric lot up there. Were you caught trying to cross Hadrian's Wall?' asked the boy sympathetically.

Max was wondering how to answer when the boy added, 'Enough of the chatter! There's no time for idleness with a banquet to prepare. Come. You can give me a hand with the basket. It's needed in the kitchen.'

Max stared at the boy. What should he do? He didn't want to go to the kitchen, where there would be lots of people and more chance of discovery. Slowly, as he backed down the ladder, a simple plan formed in his head. He would grab Dixie and make a run for it back to the lift. But Dixie had disappeared. Max stared at the basket. Was she hiding among the cherries or had she climbed out and gone somewhere else?

'Hurry up,' said the boy. 'We'll get a beating if we're too long.'

There was nothing for it. Max took one handle of the basket and reluctantly helped the boy to carry it back to the kitchen. He needn't have worried about being discovered. The kitchen was hot and crowded, with too many people all rushing around.

'Put that there, then go fetch me some lettuce,' snapped a hassled-looking cook wearing a three-quarters-length tunic. 'And be quick.'

Max stared at the basket of cherries. This was a good chance to escape, but where was Dixie? Max couldn't leave without the dormouse.

'I'm going to the garden to get some lettuce,' he said loudly, in case Dixie was in the basket and could hear him.

The cook eyed him suspiciously.

'Just get on with it,' she snapped.

Max stared at the basket once more and saw that the cherries were moving. They rolled over each other like glossy red marbles as something pushed its way through them. A twitchy nose followed by long whiskers appeared.

'About time too,' said Max, bending

down and scooping Dixie into his hand. 'Been enjoying yourself, have you?'

'Keep your tail on,' said Dixie. 'It was no picnic in there.'

'No?' Max chuckled, wiping a smear of cherry juice from Dixie's face. 'Course it wasn't.'

'Oi,' shouted a short girl in a dirty tunic, pointing an accusing finger at Max. 'The new boy's got a fatty mouse. He stole it from the pot.'

'Fatty mouse! Huh!' squeaked Dixie, indignantly.

Max burst out laughing, but the kitchen fell silent and everyone stared at him. Bang! The hassled-looking cook slammed her knife into the table.

'No one steals from my kitchen,' she roared. 'Here, boy, now!'

'Stealing?' Max shot a furious look at the

girl in the grubby tunic. 'I wasn't stealing. I caught a dormouse eating the cherries and I was putting her outside.'

'Why?' asked the cook, staring at Max.

Max returned her gaze without even blinking. 'Because that's where she belongs.'

'You're new, aren't you? Then I'll give you the benefit of the doubt. Give me the fatty mouse. It belongs in this pot.'

Max let out a tiny sigh of relief as the cook pointed to a large clay pot high on a shelf. Max's brain buzzed as he tried to remember why the Ancient Romans would keep dormice in a clay pot.

'Galloping gladiators!' he hissed, suddenly recalling the reason.

Dormice, or fatty mice as

they called them, were a delicacy in Roman times. They were kept in clay pots until they were nice and plump, then they were cooked. If he handed Dixie over, she would be roasted and eaten at the banquet. Max closed his hand protectively around his little friend. Stroppy as she was, he couldn't help liking her. Besides, he was the pet sitter. There was no way he was handing over his latest responsibility.

'Hurry, boy,' snapped the woman.

'I'll put her back,' said Max, stalling for time.

'You! You're far too short to reach.' The woman laughed. 'Give the fatty mouse here, then go and fetch the lettuce.'

Max started towards her then suddenly he gave a blood-curdling yell and gently dropped Dixie on the floor.

'Ouch! She bit me!'

Clutching his finger, Max gave an award-winning performance of pretending to be in pain.

'Clumsy oaf!' shrieked the cook. 'Don't just stand there. Catch it!'

Dirty Tunic took off, shoving past Max to chase after Dixie.

'Snitch,' Max muttered, thinking he'd like to shove her in a pot for roasting.

Several of the younger slaves also downed

their tools to join in the chase, while the older ones shook their heads and carried on working. Desperately Max elbowed people out of the way. He had to reach Dixie before anyone else did. But Dixie was whizzing around and around the kitchen like a firecracker and no one could get near her. She darted across the feet of a boy who then slipped on a tomato and crashed to the ground. A second boy tripped over him, pulling Dirty Tunic down with him.

'Wicked!' cheered Max, avoiding the pile-up.

Dixie squeezed behind a tall clay jar as the slaves on the floor struggled to get up.

'Where did it go?'

'It was there a minute ago.'

'It went that way.'

Max sidled over to the jar and squatted down beside it.

'Dixie,' he hissed, 'it's me. Max. Climb on to my hand and I'll get you out of here.'

'No,' said Dixie hotly. 'There's a whole bunch of my relatives in that pot. I'm not leaving without freeing them.'

'You're not going to try and rescue them? Dixie, you can't! It's far too dangerous. We have to get back to the lift before there's real trouble.'

'Go without me then.'

'Don't tempt me,' said Max.

'I'm not going anywhere until I've saved my relations,' said Dixie. 'You wouldn't.'

Max thought about his relatives, and an image of Alice making fun of him in front of all her friends floated into his head. Would he risk his life to save Alice? Annoying as she was, Max knew he probably would.

'All right,' he said. 'Climb on my hand and I'll help you rescue them.'

CHAPTER SEVEN
STUCK IN TIME

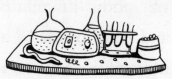

Dixie clambered into Max's hand and he closed his fingers around her soft little body. Half a second later he was surrounded by Dirty Tunic and a bunch of slaves.

'Where did the mouse go?' asked one. 'Did you see it?'

'It went that way,' said Max.

He chuckled as the slaves rushed to the other side of the kitchen, then casually he sauntered over to the shelf where the earthenware pot stood. No one noticed. The older slaves were busy with their work. The younger ones were searching for Dixie in a basket of tomatoes. Max pulled himself up on to the wooden table directly below the shelf. The table wobbled, and Max grabbed at the shelf to steady himself. The clay pot was heavy and Max needed both hands to lift it down. He was so busy trying not to drop it that when the table wobbled again Max fell back, landing on his bottom with the clay pot in his lap. His hand flew to his pocket and felt for Dixie, then he grinned as she tickled him with her tail. That was close. He'd have to be more careful. The jar would have given Dixie more than a headache if it had landed on her!

Dirty Tunic was crawling around on the floor. If she looked up now she would see Max sitting on the table. Quietly Max lay the jar on its side and eased the lid off. He angled the jar away from himself, expecting the dormice to rush out, but nothing happened. Max stuck his hand inside the jar and his fingers sank into a mass of velvety bodies. Even then they didn't stir.

'Dixie, help me,' Max whispered.

Dixie wriggled out of his pocket, climbed on to the jar and stuck her head inside. She began squeaking very fast in dormouse language. Seconds later the jar erupted with orange fur balls as a dozen fat dormice scampered to safety. As

they fled they knocked the lid to the ground and it smashed on the stone floor. Dirty Tunic spun round.

'You!' she cried, standing up. 'You've let all the fatty mice go.'

Max grabbed Dixie and scrambled down from the table, but the cook had seen him.

'Clumsy!' she yelled, boxing Max on the ear. 'Catch them now or I'll be roasting you instead.'

Max fled across the kitchen and outside. Dirty Tunic followed as Max dodged around the statues to the part of the garden where they'd left the lift.

'Stop!' cried Dirty Tunic.

'In your dreams,' shouted Max.

The lift was where he'd remembered – sandwiched between two willowy trees. Max threw himself at it, slamming his hand

on the buttons outside. The doors slid open.
Max ran in, flipped open the hidden control
panel and pressed the >< button.

'Hooray!' he cheered as the lift closed.

'What is this place?' asked a voice.

Max spun round. Dirty Tunic had
followed him into the lift.

'Get out,' he said, shoving her backwards.

'Shan't.'

'Get out!' yelled Max, shoving her harder.

Dirty Tunic leaned against the lift doors. 'I can't. The door's disappeared. This place is so strange.'

'Bye-bye,' said Max.

He pushed a button, the doors slid open and Dirty Tunic fell backwards into the garden.

'You can't hide in there forever,' she shouted as the doors closed again.

Max slumped against the lift wall to catch his breath.

'Dixie, what do we press to get home?' he asked. 'Is it the F button? F for future, right?'

Dixie crouched on the floor and her long black whiskers trembled.

'It's not that simple,' she said.

'Well, make it simple,' yelled Max. 'We haven't got much time.'

Dixie quivered. 'I can't. I was going to tell you earlier.'

'Tell me what?' Max felt uneasy. What hadn't Dixie told him?

'We can't get back. The lift isn't finished. The time dial needs a pointer so you can pick the exact date you want to travel to. Ivor's friend Tor was making a special one carved from oak. Ivor was so excited when Tor emailed to say that the pointer was ready. That's why he went away, to collect the pointer.'

Max stared at Dixie in disbelief. After a minute he asked, 'So how did we get here?'

'Pot luck,' Dixie replied. 'Pressing F takes you somewhere into the future. Pressing P takes you back into the past. You just can't set an exact date.'

'Nice!' exploded Max. 'Why didn't you tell this me before?'

'You were more interested in going off to find the cherries,' said Dixie.

'What! The cherries were your idea.' Max's green eyes narrowed to tiny slits.

'All right!' said Dixie sounding a tiny bit embarrassed. 'I decided to keep it for later. I think better on a full stomach.'

Max felt his heart beat faster as he thought about their predicament. They could be stuck in the wrong time forever.

'OK!' he said slowly. His heart was still racing and he felt slightly out of breath. 'What happens now?'

'We press the F button and hope for the best. Wherever we go, it can't be worse than this place,' Dixie shuddered. 'Roasted dormouse! That's bad!'

It wasn't the answer Max wanted, but Dixie was right. Travelling nearer to their own time had to be less dangerous than being stuck in Ancient Roman times. Then

Max had an idea. What if they had a makeshift time-dial pointer? Might that get them back to their own time?

'What does the pointer look like? Could we make one?'

'It's got a round bottom and a long pointy stick like a speed dial in a car,' said Dixie.

Max glanced at Dixie's fat little body and her long tail, then grinned.

'No way!' squeaked Dixie, reading his mind. 'You are not using me!' A sudden pounding on the door made Max and Dixie jump.

'Open up!' bellowed a man's voice.

The pounding continued until the lift doors burst open. A surprised-looking man in a long white tunic stared in. Dirty Tunic was with him, and she was fiddling with the lift controls.

'That's him,' she said, smugly.

Quickly Max pushed the >< button and the doors slid closed again. He kept his finger on the button to keep them shut, ignoring the angry shouts from outside.

Think! What could you use for a makeshift time-dial pointer? Unusually Max's pockets were empty except for his pet sitter's notebook and pencil. Max stared around the lift, but apart from himself and Dixie it was completely empty. Then he had an idea. His pencil would make a good pointer and the button on his trousers was round! Using his free hand Max unfastened his button and tried to pull it off. The button was stitched so firmly in place that it didn't even move.

'Dixie,' said Max, 'can you nibble this free for me?'

'Good idea,' said Dixie. 'You're going to use it for a pointer.'

Quickly she scampered up Max's leg and sunk her teeth into the cotton. Max giggled.

'That tickles!'

The pounding on the door grew more violent.

'Open up. Open up at once or I'll feed you to the lions!'

'Careful!' chuckled Max. 'Your whiskers are soooo tickly!'

'Paaa!' Dixie spat a mouthful of cotton, then triumphantly passed Max the button. 'It goes in that hole,' she said.

'I know,' said Max, having already worked out that the hole in the control panel was where the time-dial pointer should be.

Max threaded the button through the dangling wire with his free hand. It was far too small, but it would have to do. Next he fastened the pencil to it, using the end of the wire. He gave it a twist, cheering as the pencil spun around.

'Ready?' he asked Dixie.

'Ready,' she agreed, climbing into his pocket.

Max thought for a

moment. He wasn't sure how far to turn the pencil. Roman times had been around two thousand years ago, so he'd better give it a good twist. The pounding outside was replaced by a metallic-sounding twang as if someone was attacking the lift with an axe. Hurriedly Max turned the pencil three-quarters of the way round, then slammed his hand on the F button. For a second nothing happened, then the lift suddenly shot sideways then upwards.

'Hooray!' cheered Max, grabbing the handrail as the spinning began.

CHAPTER EIGHT
INTO THE FUTURE

The spinning lasted for longer this time. Max gripped the rail until his hands were numb from holding on. He could feel Dixie's warm little body in his pocket, and he hoped that she was all right. When at last the spinning stopped, Max waited, ready for the sudden plunge downwards. But the time lift was full of surprises.

'Eeeek!' he shouted as they shot upwards.

Max wasn't sure which was worse: the feeling of falling or this new feeling of whizzing into space. Neither, he decided. It was this bit: the sudden jolt as the lift bounced itself to a standstill. This was a hundred times worse than anything else. Max's bones felt as if they were about to come crashing through his skin. He closed his eyes until at last the lift stilled and the doors finally slid open.

'Phew!' he cried, seeing they were downstairs in Ivor's hall. 'We made it! How lucky was that?'

Eagerly Dixie scrambled from Max's pocket.

'Listen!' Max caught her as she scampered down his leg. 'What's that noise?'

Cautiously he stuck his head out of the lift, then quickly pulled it back in. Who was the old man with the long grey hair shuffling down the hall? Ivor hadn't said that anyone else would be visiting Dixie. Coughing and wheezing, the man shuffled closer.

'Who's there?' he called. 'I thought I heard something.

82

Who is it?'

'Ivor!' squeaked Dixie. 'What happened?'

Something clicked in Max's brain.

'Dozy dormice!' he exclaimed. 'We've overshot. We've travelled into the future.'

Quickly he shut the lift doors, then reaching up he twisted the pencil back a little and hit the Past button.

'Let's hope this does it,' he muttered as the lift began to spin.

Anxiously Max waited. What if he'd turned the pointer too far? They could be travelling backwards and forwards forever. Seconds later the ride was over and the lift doors opened. Tentatively Max looked out.

They were back in Ivor's house, in the upstairs room they had started from. 'We did it! We're home!' Max cheered. He checked his watch – they'd been gone an hour, although it seemed much longer. Hitching up his shorts, which were slipping down his skinny waist, he triumphantly carried Dixie out of the lift.

CHAPTER NINE
HOME AGAIN

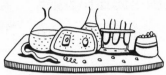

Max and Dixie were having a water fight with Dixie's water bottles. Dixie had shown Max how to make the spout twist around and squirt water, but she was still getting the better of him as she was expert at hiding.

'Mouse-eye!' shouted Dixie, leaping from behind a tyre and blasting Max in the face.

'I'll get you for that,' laughed Max, wiping water from his eyes.

'Not if I get you first,' shrieked Dixie, blasting Max again.

Max ducked and fired back, soaking Dixie's long furry tail as she nipped behind an old computer.

'Mouse-eye!' he yelled.

'Hold fire!' Dixie's
head popped round the
computer, her ears
twitching.

'Yeah, right!' laughed Max,
blasting her again. 'I'm not that
stupid!'

'No, really. That was the door. Quick,
Ivor's home!'

Dixie ran back to her cage. Max dropped
his water bottle and frantically mopped up
the mess. He managed to clear up most of
the water before Ivor came in to the room.

'Hello,' said Max, stuffing a wad of wet
tissue into his pocket.

'Hello,' said Ivor, looking around. 'It's a
bit damp in here. Is everything all right?'

'Everything's fine,' said Max.

'Couldn't be finer,' called Dixie from her villa.

Ivor looked at them both suspiciously.

'Good to see you two so friendly,' he said eventually. 'Dixie behaved herself, did she? She wasn't talking to you when I left.'

'Dixie's been very good,' said Max.

'What about him?' Ivor looked at Dixie.

'The best pet sitter ever,' said Dixie.

'I knew he would be.' Ivor dumped his suitcase on top of the broken guitar, then let Dixie out of her cage.

'Did you have an enjoyable trip?' asked Max politely.

'Oh yes,' Ivor's eyes flicked to his suitcase. 'The trip went very

well. The time just flew by. I can't believe I've been away for three whole days. I'll be an old man, little and bald, before I know it.'

Max and Dixie chuckled.

'Old maybe, but bald . . . I don't think so.' Dixie winked at Max.

Ivor tweaked his long ponytail.

'Maybe not bald,' he agreed.

'Old and grey?' suggested Max.

Ivor gave him a sharp look, but Max was already hurrying for the door.

'I'll be off then,' he called. 'See you around Dixie. Bye Ivor.'

'Bye Max,' said Dixie. 'See you sometime in the future, maybe!'

Me and Dixie!

ABOUT THE AUTHOR

Julie Sykes has had more than thirty books published including several about her creation, Little Tiger. Among her other titles are *That Pesky Dragon*, *Dora's Eggs* and *Hurry, Santa!*

I Don't Want to Go to Bed! and *I Don't Want to Have a Bath!* won the Nottingham Children's Book Award. Julie has three children and lives in Hampshire.

ABOUT THE ILLUSTRATOR

Nathan Reed has illustrated children's stories for Puffin, HarperCollins and Campbell Books. He also illustrated one of the most popular titles in Kingfisher's *I Am Reading* series, *Hocus Pocus Hound*. Nathan lives in London.